NICOLA DAVIES
THE WHITE HARE

ILLUSTRATIONS ANASTASIA IZLESOU

for Jackie Morris

GRAFFEG

NICOLA DAVIES
THE WHITE HARE

ILLUSTRATIONS ANASTASIA IZLESOU

The White Hare
First published in Great Britain in
2016 by Graffeg Limited.
This paperback edition published
in 2020 by Graffeg Limited.

Written by Nicola Davies
copyright © 2016.
Illustrated by Anastasia Izlesou
copyright © 2016.
This edition designed and produced by
Graffeg Limited copyright © 2020.

Graffeg Limited, 24 Stradey Park
Business Centre, Mwrwg Road,
Llangennech, Llanelli, Carmarthenshire,
SA14 8YP, Wales, UK.
Tel 01554 824000. www.graffeg.com.

ISBN 9781913733476

2 3 4 5 6 7 8 9

THE WHITE HARE

In the days before computers, before cars, before electricity in wires or water in taps, or food in supermarkets, before even roads and writing, people lived by what they could get from the land. Humans were closer to nature, at the mercy of the cold and wind, floods and drought, as other animals were. Humans and animals were fellow beings under the sky. Perhaps that's why it seemed possible, back then, for humans to change into animals, and animals into humans.

In those times there lived a girl called Ostra, in a village by the sea. Not a village as we think of them now, with a stone church, a pub, a village green; more a collection of huts, shelters made of wood and stones, mud and animal skins, huddled at the foot of a cliff. People ate what they could take from the sea or from the woods above the clifftops.

There were a few fields of crops perhaps, maybe even some skinny little sheep, a few ponies, but that's all. There were no rabbits then either, just long, lean hares, running on the heathery heaths and the clifftops where trees wouldn't grow. Running under the moon, wild as the wind and full of magic.

Ostra's life had no magic in it at all. She was the eldest of five children. There had been more but most children died before they could walk back then, so Ostra's brothers and sisters were already tough survivors. Their mother was dead and their father spent all day out in his boat trying to get them enough fish to eat, so Ostra did pretty much everything else. Cooking, sweeping, making clothes, wiping snotty noses, scolding, nagging, cuddling. And one other job too, which was making her father's crab pots. No plastic of course, so she wove the pots from the long bendy stems of willow.

Weaving pots was a winter job. In spring and summer willow stems lose their bendiness and become snappy and brittle. So, on winter evenings, after it was dark and her father was back from the sea, Ostra walked up the cliff to the marshy willow bed on the edge of the woods to cut the willow stems and weave them. She worked by the light of the moon or of a little rush lantern, yellow-flamed and trailing the stink of animal fat. In the cold, in the wind, in the rain.

Ostra liked the work, because it was peaceful and solitary and gave her time to be quiet.

The rhythm of bending and binding the stems to make the big, open shape of the crab pot pleased her. Sometimes she sang quietly to herself, but more often she sat quietly listening to the sounds of the winter night; the screaming vixens, the owls hooting, the wolves howling and, above all the sounds of Earth, to the big silence of the stars. Listening in the cold, winter silence is how she came to hear animals speaking to her.

One still, frosty night, as she sat bending the willow stems with her strong determined hands, a robin came and landed on the ground at her feet. Its feathers were so fluffed out against the freezing night that it looked like a little ball standing on two skinny legs, like wires.

"You got any food, missis?" the robin asked in its tiny, ringing voice.

"Only a crust," Ostra replied, before she had time to think that she was holding a conversation with a bird. Whether it had really spoken or she was just too tired to think straight, didn't seem to matter anyway. It was pretty clear that, on a cold night like this, it was only right to share whatever you had with other living creatures. So she broke a crust to crumbs and scattered them on the ground for the little bird.

"Fanks, missis," said the robin, through the crumbs, because no one teaches robins not to speak with their beaks full. Then it flew away saying, "You won't be sorry!"

Ostra returned to her pot making and told herself she must be hearing things.

But a week or two later, it happened again. She sat bending the stems under the stars like always, when a wren landed on the ground in front of her.

"I'm sooo cold, missis!" it said, its voice tinier and higher even than the robin's.

"Well come here and I'll warm you!" Ostra replied, as usual thinking of how she could help before she thought about anything else. She opened her hands and the bird came and sat between them, while Ostra breathed warmth under its feathers.

"Thanks, missis!" said the bird as it flew off, "you won't be sorry."

Ostra shook her head, convinced she'd fallen asleep over her work, which was pretty likely as with all she had to do, she was always tired. Back home she was too busy carrying wood, making fires, cleaning fish, fetching water, picking lice out of hair, sewing skins, scolding, nagging and cuddling to even remember that she had thought she'd heard a bird say words.

Yet, every few nights throughout the winter, as she made her pots, some little bird or mouse, some small, small helpless thing of the forest would come and ask for her help. And it was always the same, before she even thought, she gave whatever help was asked for because that was her nature. The response, too, was always the same.

"Thanks, missis, you won't be sorry!" they called out in parting in a voice as small as a raindrop.

So Ostra had to accept that she could hold a conversation with a small creature, even though that ability seemed to make no difference whatever to the harshness of her life.

She was still fetching, carrying, cooking, cleaning, scolding, nagging and cuddling and generally worrying over far too many other people, including her father, who was so tired when he got in from his boat that all he could do was snore.

And so it went on.

But somebody else had noticed what a kind, reliable, hardworking girl Ostra was. Wolvas, the hunter. His special skill was killing things. Stabbing, strangling, trapping or poisoning. And then he ate what he killed, wore its skin or traded its body for something else he wanted. Wolvas had seen Ostra working and working away in those winter nights, her strong hands bending the willow, and he wanted all that hard work and strength for himself.

So, come springtime, when other jobs replaced pot making, Wolvas came looking for Ostra one morning when she was up at dawn collecting young nettle heads for soup. He jumped out of a bush and greeted her.

Now I should say here that Wolvas was considered to be very, very good looking, so Ostra was pretty pleased when he said, "Ostra, I'd like to make you my wife!"

She was all set to blush and say, "Oh, all right then!" but a little robin landed on her shoulder and whispered into her ear, "He's wicked and cruel. Tell him no."

Ostra noticed then, a string of robins, freshly killed and hanging from his belt by their tiny, wiry legs and dripping red jewels of blood from their delicate beaks onto his leather trousers.

So she did what the bird asked.

"No," she told the huntsman, "I can't marry while my littlest brother has a cough."

Wolvas tried to put a good face on it, but he was handsome and he wasn't used to women turning him down. He stomped off into the forest using words that Ostra had never heard anyone say!

Two weeks later, Ostra's little brother suddenly

took a turn for the worse, and died in the night. Wolvas came and found Ostra as she laid wild flowers on the little boy's grave.

"Ostra," he said, "I'd like to make you my wife."

Ostra was so upset about her brother that the thought of being held in the huntsman's big strong arms made her want to say, "YES!" But before she could get the word out, a little wren landed on her shoulder and said, "He's wicked and cruel, tell him no!"

That's when Ostra noticed that the huntsman wore a necklace of a hundred baby birds, small and naked as peas, hanging around his neck like pink beads.

So she did what the bird asked, "No," she said, "I can't marry until my sisters are old enough to keep house."

Once again the huntsman stomped off into the woods, furious. Two weeks later, Ostra's little sisters were down on the beach in the sunshine collecting driftwood for the fire. One second they were there, and the next they were gone. Ostra, her brother, her father and all the villagers searched and searched, but the girls had vanished into thin air. Swept out to sea by a freak wave, folk said, but the sea was calm and no bodies washed up with tide.

Ostra was grief stricken. Although there was less work to do now, she cried over the three fewer mouths to feed, and fewer little bodies to clothe and fuss over, to care for and cuddle.

Still the work and the caring for her one remaining brother and her father had to go on, so one summer night she walked up the hill and onto the clifftop to gather sweet marjoram and bedstraw to put on the floor of the hut to keep it smelling nice (and to keep the fleas under control).

Wolvas, the huntsman, came and found her yet again. His handsome face was tanned and his strong arms were bare and bronzed, his big

blue eyes were the colour of the sea. Ostra felt her knees going quite wobbly.

"Ostra, now will you be my wife?"

How Ostra longed to say yes!

But a tiny harvest mouse, gold as the sunshine, ran out of the grass and up onto Ostra's shoulder. It squeaked into her ear, "He's wicked and cruel, tell him no!"

That's when Ostra noticed that the handsome waistcoat that covered – but only just – the huntsman's broad chest was made of hundreds and hundreds of harvest mouse skins.

"No, I can't," she told Wolvas, "my brother and my father need me to cook for them."

This time the huntsman didn't even try to conceal his fury. He kicked trees, he snapped branches and he stomped away with a very unattractive expression on his face.

And two weeks later, on the stillest, hottest, bluest morning of all the summer, Ostra's father took his last young son to sea, to teach him how to set a crab pot. Anxiously, Ostra watched the two figures in the fragile, little craft. She was still watching, helpless, as the boat sank below the shining surface, quite suddenly, as if it had sprung a leak and filled with water.

Ostra felt she had snapped like a willow stem. She turned from the village and lay on the clifftop on the warm breast of the earth, weeping, weeping. The day waned and the sky changed colour and still she wept. There Wolvas found her and pulled her roughly to her feet.

"Ostra," he said, "you have no family and no protection. Now surely you must take me as your husband."

Ostra wiped her eyes and looked at him. For the first time she saw that he wasn't handsome at all: that he had a nasty, hard mouth; that his eyes were like a dead fish's, and his muscly body was rather stringy and cold. So when a

beautiful brown hare popped his head out of the undergrowth and started to say, "He's wi..."

Ostra interrupted the creature, "I know, I know!" she told the hare. "But I've got no more excuses!"

"Then," the hare told her, "you must run!"

A tiny bubble of light rose up in the dark of Ostra's heart at the hare's words. She leapt away with an energy that surprised her and completely astonished Wolvas. In a moment she was racing along the clifftop, following the loping hare, past the osier bed, through the woods and out the other side. The hare and Ostra ran and ran, out at last onto the wide, heathery heath, under the sky and the wild wind.

And that's where Wolvas the huntsman caught her. His long legs stretched out and his sinewy arm reached and caught her by the wrist, squeezing, wicked and cruel. Not a shred of handsomeness or even humanity was left in

his face as he told Ostra, "I poisoned your little
brother and still you refused me!" Wolvas cried,
"I strangled your sisters and buried them under
the sand, and still you refused me. I holed your
father's boat and watched him drown with your
brother, and still you refused me. Do you think
I'll hesitate to break your neck if you refuse me
again?"

Ostra didn't know what to say. She was full of
fear and flamed with fury. But she didn't need to
say a word because a cloud was gathering over the
huntsman's head and a moving carpet under his
feet. A cloud and carpet of tiny helpless creatures,
hundreds and hundreds and hundreds of little
beaks and little claws and little teeth, sharp and
fierce.

Like a tide, quiet and quick, they covered the
huntsman, pecking and tearing and biting.

"Ostra, Ostra!" called the hare, from behind

her, "You can leave that all behind you now. Turn around and come with me," he said, "you won't be sorry."

Ostra did as he asked. She turned around and ran after the hare, with the bubble of light inside her growing and growing until it reached the tips of her toes and the top of her head. She ran on, faster and faster. Running out the tiredness, and grief and anger and fear. Running into the beautiful summer night, under the silence of the stars, until all she could feel was the air in her lungs and the sweet springy turf, beneath her four, white furry feet.

Nicola Davies

Nicola is an award-winning author, whose many books for children include *The Promise* (Green Earth Book Award 2015, CILIP Kate Greenaway Medal Shortlist 2015), *Tiny* (AAAS/Subaru SB&F Prize 2015), *A First Book of Nature, Whale Boy* (Blue Peter Book Awards Shortlist 2014), and the Heroes of the Wild series (Portsmouth Book Award 2014).

She graduated in Zoology, studied whales and bats and then worked for the BBC Natural History Unit. Underlying all Nicola's writing is the belief that a relationship with nature is essential to every human being, and that now, more than ever, we need to renew that relationship.

Nicola's children's books from Graffeg include *Perfect, The Pond*, the Shadows and Light series, *The Word Bird, Animal Surprises, Into the Blue* and *Secret of the Egg*.

Anastasia Izlesou

Anastasia Izlesou is a UK based freelance illustrator from Lithuania. She studied illustration at the Arts University Bournemouth. Her preferred media are watercolour and pencil. Anastasia's deep interest in literature and nature informs and inspires her illustration practice.

   The White Hare is Anastasia's first published book.

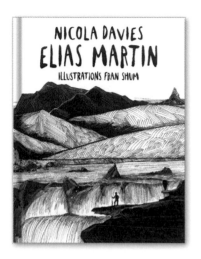

The White Hare by Nicola Davies
Illustrated by Anastasia Izlesou
Print and eBook editions.

Back then, humans and animals were
fellow beings under the sky. Perhaps
that's why it seemed possible for
humans to change into animals.

'The White Hare is a really interesting
fairy tale, and it makes you realize how
close we all are to the animals.
The book has beautiful illustrations,
that are dreamlike but kind of sad and
dark, even though there are some that
are very colorful.'
**Rachel Wagner, San Diego Book
Review**

Elias Martin by Nicola Davies
Illustrated by Fran Shum
Print and eBook editions.

**Elias Martin lives a scowling, solitary
life for a decade until a small, lost
child wanders into his path.**

'Elias Martin lives a lonely, isolated life
in the middle of a snowy forest. Then
one day he finds a strange young child
sleeping in his wood store, and he soon
takes the child under his wing. Davies
is inspired by both nature and grim
folklore in this tale. Shum's beautiful
black-and-white illustrations perfectly
complement Davies's writing, especially
emphasising the starkness of the harsh
landscape. A mysterious and highly
engrossing read.'
**Inis Reading Guide 2017-18,
Children's Books Ireland**

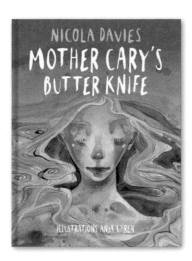

Mother Cary's Butter Knife
by Nicola Davies
Illustrated by Anja Uhren
Print and eBook editions.

The smallest of three brothers, Keenan Mowat had a priceless talent: he loved the sea and the sea loved him right back.

'The book is short, but will immerse you in its story, and the illustrations add to the mystical and otherwordly feel. Mother Cary's Butter Knife by Nicola Davies and Anja Uhren is a new fairy tale that already feels like a classic.'
San Diego Book Review

The Selkie's Mate
by Nicola Davies
Illustrated by Claire Jenkins
Print and eBook editions.

In a land where people flow between ocean and land, a seal and a fisherman sing together under a glowing moon. When the beautiful selkie comes to live ashore, the fisherman must promise to let her one day return to the sea.

'Lyrical text is enhanced by evocative watercolour illustrations in this heart-wrenching tale of love, loss and trust. Inspired by Selkie legends from around the world, this haunting story is part of the Shadows and Light series, ideal for mature readers who are looking for something a bit different.'
BookTrust's Watery Reads for 8-12s

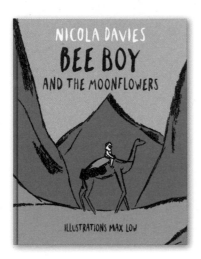

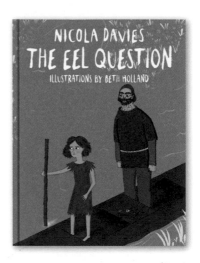

Bee Boy and the Moonflowers
by Nicola Davies
Illustrated by Max Low
Print and eBook editions.

Azin and his nomadic family rely upon the Moonflowers to keep them alive. When his elders are taken ill, young Azin is left to guide the bees to these rare flowers and return with their precious honey, but he is not the only one seeking out their magic...

'These stories ask as many questions as they answer and highlight the strong ties that exist between nature and mankind; they beg us to seek a little deeper. Thought-provoking, haunting and swimming with the diverse beauty of the natural world.'
Mary Esther Judy, Fallen Star Stories

The Eel Question
by Nicola Davies
Illustrated by Beth Holland
Print and eBook editions.

Bound to serve a cruel master, Nant's curiosity never fails to get her into trouble. Her dreams of a life beyond her marshland home intensify each autumn when the silver eels return, along with her questions. Where do they come from? And where do they go?

'This unusual, mythic-feeling story is one of a series of tales from Welsh publisher Graffeg that explore the deeper and sometimes darker side of our connection with the natural world. Nant finds herself at the mercy of a witch hunt, and the story explores themes of ignorance and curiosity with a deft and gentle hand.' **BookTrust**